IRISH PLAYS AND OTHERS; Volume 4

RIVERMAN

a play by Sam Dowling

85 Haddo House
Haddo Street
LONDON SE10 9SE

E-mail <praxis.lab@ntlworld.com>

Published by Lulu 2007

www.lulu.com

ISBN 978-1-84753-699-0

SAM DOWLING

Is a Dublin-born playwright. He has written and produced nearly thirty plays or small-cast versions of classics for Praxis Theatre Laboratory. His subject-matter has ranged from Irish history through the lives of writers and artists to re-working of themes from the Greek myths. His play about the Brontës (co-written with Andrea Bird) has had three productions in Tokyo.
For more detail see listing in playwrights' database www.doollee.com

PRAXIS THEATRE LABORATORY is an experimental theatre which seeks its direction from the actors' response to the work. No-one takes on a separate role as director. We particularly value images conjured in rehearsal, and intuitive and emotional rather than intellectual or technical evaluation. We try to fix as little as possible and each performance retains an element of improvisation.
Founded by Sam Dowling as the in-house company at The Tabard in West London from 1984, in 1990 we left to pursue more experimental goals. We opened a small theatre space in County Roscommon, Ireland in 1999 and have toured UK, USA, Ireland, Belgium, Netherlands, Ukraine and Poland.

RIVERMAN was first performed at The Tabard Theatre in Turnham Green, London, on 6 June 1985. with this cast:

GREAVES........................Stephen Bateman
TINNIE........................ Hilary Sesta
MARCHANT........................Trevor Ainsley
SPENCER........................Eve Shickle
Joseph PENNELL........................Michael Jayes
Elizabeth PENNELL........................Sara Squires
Augustus JOHN........................Robbin John
JENNY........................Eve Shickle

Directed by Jeremy Browne
Designed by Steve Williams Produced by Niamh Dowling
Music composed and recorded by Andrea Black.
In later productions Joseph PENNELL omitted.

For performance permission and terms, contact Sam Dowling.

IRISH PLAYS AND OTHERS BY SAM DOWLING IN PRINT OR IN THE PIPELINE

RIVERMAN [*Walter Greaves, naïf painter, rise and fall.*]
CAULDRON OF BRONTËS [*Genius siblings.*]
A SEASON IN HELL [Wild poets Rimbaud and Verlaine.]
MOUNTAIN [Life-changing encounters]
RENEWAL [Site-specific version of MOUNTAIN]
TROJAN WOMEN
BIRTH OF THE BEAST [Northern Ireland.]
BIG FELLA! [Michael Collins.]
ALLEGIANCE [IRA in London.]
ANTIGONE
THE FLAME AND THE STONE [Yeats and Maud Gonne.]
VIRGIN OF NOTTING HILL [Sexual problems.]
ORESTEIAN TRILOGY
LOVELOST [Abuse]
RED COUNTESS GREEN CROW [Markievicz and O'Casey]
HA! HA! HA! [Improvisations on Coward and Shakespeare.]

AND SMALL-CAST VERSIONS OF THESE CLASSICS;

THE CENCI
IMPORTANCE OF BEING EARNEST
CHERRY ORCHARD
THREE SISTERS
HEDDA GABLER
WHEN WE DEAD AWAKEN
HAMLET
MACBETH
ANTONY AND CLEOPATRA
THE TEMPEST

DRAMATIS PERSONAE

WALTER GREAVES
TINNIE GREAVES
AUGUSTUS JOHN
ELIZABETH PENNELL
WILLIAM MARCHANT
SARAH SPENCER
JENNY

The play is set in London 1910- 1911

The set will be required to accommodate
or suggest The Embankment, Greaves's poor lodgings,
The Goupil Gallery, The Savoy, Spencer's bookshop

RIVERMAN

PART ONE

[London 1910;
The Embankment at Cheyne Walk.
GREAVES setting out his wares on
a clear cold winter's morning in the
forlorn hope of selling something
to passers-by. Enter JENNY hurrying along.]

GREAVES
Fancy one of these Lady ? It's all good work
Two and six the watercolours five for ten shillings
A pupil of Whistler's I was...

JENNY
Morning Mr Greaves !
Perishing innit ?

GREAVES [Doffs his old topper.]
Oh good morning Jenny
Madame Strindberg keeping well ?

JENNY
Very well thank you kindly
She killed herself again and never touched her breakfast
I've to fetch Mr John to her

GREAVES
She does put you through it don't she !

JENNY
All in a day's work and lucky to have it these days
As Madame likes to remind me
Well see yah later !

[Exit JENNY.
Enter JOHN and MARCHANT]

MARCHANT
Cheyne Walk !
The gardens ran right down to the river here before they built the Embankment
Turner lived in that end house...Wilde there... Whistler of course.. Rossetti
All facing South in the summer sunshine...can you imagine ?
Swinbourne and the others hurrying along to seventy-four
For Whistler's brilliant breakfasts on the lawn !
Carlyle tottering on to World's End for his snuff or whatever

JOHN
I detest artists
So damned narrow-minded

MARCHANT
A new century !
You can sniff something in the air !

JOHN
The tide is out

MARCHANT
Excitement ! London is ready for something new
A sensation ! It's there and there's a fortune to be made from it !
This new Georgian era will be kind to the artist Augustus

JOHN
Oh I'm coining it in as it is
Cheques and fifty pound notes littered all over my studio...
There must be something fundamentally wrong with my work

MARCHANT
Nothing wrong with being paid for one's labours
Even if one is an artist ! Ha ha ha !

JOHN
Or being paid for someone else's labours if you're an art dealer eh Marchant ? Ha ha ha !

MARCHANT
I work hard for every penny I make

JOHN
Someone works hard for every pound you make ! Ha ha ha 1

MARCHANT
A man must join the winners or the losers
I snatched and took the future in my hands...

JOHN
Last night I met a little girl down Chelsea
In filthy dustbins poking round for food...

MARCHANT
It's dog eat dog and piss upon the failure
Your stature is your balance in the bank...

JOHN
I filled her in the caff with meat and brandy
And screwed her in the lane behind the church

MARCHANT
Yes that's the measure of a man
And the pleasure of a man
And of it's all done in the name of Art..

JOHN
And if I paint her this evening as Aphrodite
And if she doesn't cry too much at parting

TOGETHER
So much the better

MARCHANT
We stand at the dawn of a new era !

JOHN

We stand at the door of The King's Head And Eight Bells

[Enter JENNY]

MARCHANT

I have a day's work to do

A bientôt [Exit]

JENNY

Oh Mr John ! Oh sir !

Madame Strindberg has killed herself

You must come at once

JOHN

Dear dear... where is she ?

JENNY

The Savoy sir

With her dying breath she says to give you this

I believe it's money sir

JOHN

Keep it

JENNY

Madame says she'll sack me if you give me the money sir

JOHN

Come on...let's see if she's really dead this time

[JOHN takes her by the waist to hurry off
when he spots a real or imagined enemy OFF]

JOHN

That fellow with you ?

JENNY

No sir he's ... Oh Mr John Madame will murder me

If we don't get there before she dies !

JOHN

How did she do it ?

JENNY

The usual sir two bottlefuls

JOHN

You get the man with the stomach-pump
And I'll bring her the comforts of...religion [Kisses her lasciviously.]

JENNY

Oh Mr John you are a one !

[Exit JOHN avoiding his 'enemy']

Any luck this morning then ?

GREAVES

Luck ! I ran out o' luck before you got out of pinafores
There's no money about

JENNY

There's money about all right
You're moving in the wrong circles Walter

GREAVES

There was always some kind of a living to made on the river in the old days
The Greaves was watermen here from way back

JENNY

I know

GREAVES

My father rowed the toffs across the river to Battersea like grandad done before
We wrought our boats by hand in Autumn sunshine
Me and me brother decorated them form stem to stern

JENNY

That was the measure of a waterman

GREAVES
And the pleasure...
And if there was a copper or two for beer of an evening
And if we sang around our old piano
And if the sister Tinnie looked lovely as a Helen or a Cleopatra...

TOGETHER
So much the better ! Ha ha ha !

JENNY
Something saucy ! That's what they want these days !
Do a lot of drawings of the Tiller girls with their skirts up over their heads
Sell like hot-cakes they would here of a Sunday afternoon

GREAVES
Oh no no no...that wouldn't do at all

JENNY
I'm telling yah !
Ay...see that there American lady's been sketching round the church ?
She was asking about you

GREAVES
Oh yes ?

JENNY
Maybe she wants to buy

GREAVES
Mrs Pennell ? She wouldn't buy nothing from me
She wrote the book about Whistler
....
No one knew more about Whistler than me... we was inseparable

JENNY
I know I know
You told us a thousand times about you and Jimmy Whistler

I could write the bleedin book meself !
Here she comes !
Touch her for half a crown Walter !

[Enter PENNELL.]

PENNELL
Ah Greaves !

GREAVES
Morning Mrs Pennell
Etching the church were you ?

PENNELL
I like the early winter light

GREAVES
Got a special way with light the Thames
Different every month

JENNY
Fancy one of Mr Greaves's pictures Miss ?
They's all brand new

PENNELL
Er... no thank you

JENNY
Tell the truth he needs for to sell something pretty sharp-like
Man is fading way to a shadda for want of a square meal
Come on ! Buy one of them little pictures for half a crown !

PENNELL
Greaves, can you give me some more of your time on the Whistler story ?

JENNY
Five shillings a day and meals

GREAVES
Of course I'll help

I though the book was all finished and printed up

PENNELL
We're working on the fifth edition

JENNY
He never works for less'n four shillings

PENNELL
I shall complain to your employer if you persist in this impertinence !
Who does she work for ?

GREAVES
No idea

JENNY [In retreat]
See you look after Walter proper that's all I'm saying [Exit]

PENNELL
Now... there are still gaps to be filled in Greaves
I am particularly anxious to include precise details of his method of working
And his use of materials
You above all knew these things... if you can still remember

GREAVES
Clear as crystal strange to say...like it was only yesterday
And the real yesterday is all confused like a dream
Hah... there's old age for you !

PENNELL
I'll give you my card...we're staying at The Savoy for a while
Can we make a start in the morning ?

GREAVES
Tomorrow ?

PENNELL
Time is money..ahem... For the publishers I mean
Tomorrow at eight-thirty say
Ah there's my automobile at last

GREAVES
It'll take me an hour-and-a-half to walk there
Yes...all right... half past eight

PENNELL
Excellent... I shall look forward to seeing you
...
Now eh Greaves... you understand eh there is no eh payment for this eh
All in the interest of history... and the memory of Whistler !

GREAVES
That's quite all right Mrs Pennell...quite all right

PENNELL
Till tomorrow then !
.....
Greaves... you are a credit to your class !
Hey driver ! You're five minutes late my friend
You're going to find yourself out of a job if y..... [Exit.]

[GREAVES, trying to keep warm , is with
his sister TINNIE in their miserable
fireless room in Fulham.
A few biscuit tins serve as furniture:
bedding of old clothes and sacks
bundled on bare floorboards.
TINNIE sits, dressed in old frippery,
cheap jewels and an improbable yellow wig.]

TINNIE
Sit down can't you ? It's making me nervous. You never sit down

GREAVES
We shouldn't have let the chair go... it's not human living like th....

TINNIE
Sit on the biscuit tin. If it's good enough for me it's...
You're such an old fool Walter Greaves
People walk on you like you was dirt
You encourage them to use you

GREAVES
Aggh...

TINNIE
Pennell will throw you in the gutter when she's finished with you
Like Whistler done before her

GREAVES
Whistler was different... he was my life...like he was yours Tinnie

TINNIE
Used us ! Used us ! Didn't want to know us when he got in with society
and all that

GREAVES
Twenty years of magic

TINNIE

He promised to marry me [GREAVES has heard this before.]
It was up to you to see he done right by me. You were my brother

GREAVES

Pennell's book is important... it's history

TINNIE

All right... but you're entitled to be paid for your history
Have no two minds about Mrs Pennell
She'll be well paid for every hour she puts into it
You owe something to yourself Walter
Last time they didn't so much as offer you a cuppa tea or a crusta bread.....

GREAVES

I told you...they don't eat till evening when their work is all done

TINNIE

Hah ! And when do we eat may I ask ?
There's neither food fire nor furniture in this house
And you go trapsing across London to work for nothing !
Tell her you need five pound or there'll be no work

GREAVES

Sssh now...

TINNIE

Five pound'd be nothing to them people... they wouldn't even miss it

GREAVES

Sssh... you'll only upset yourself
The likes of them doesn't understand the troubles of the poor

TINNIE

They understand

GREAVES

They're in a different world

TINNIE
What different world ?

GREAVES
You know what I mean

TINNIE
What different world ?

GREAVES
Get on !

TINNIE
We're in the same cursed world
Only the Pennells is warm and full of food and drink in it
And you and me is in this hell-hole cold and hungry
Scavangin with the rats over scraps of food
And God alone knows if we'll have this roof over our heads for another week
If we don't pay something off the rent...

GREAVES
I'll make a fire for you Tinnie...let's see...where's that orange box ?

TINNIE
Burned it yesterday
God I'm foundered !

GREAVES
Dear dear...I'll find something.... [Rummaging through his pictures]

TINNIE
Walter wha... ?

GREAVES
I'll make you a nice fire...

TINNIE
Walter !

GREAVES
I'll make you one nice fire !

TINNIE
WALTER !! YOU'RE NOT GOING TO BURN YOUR PICTURES !!
I'D SOONER DIE !! STOP IT !!

[GREAVES ripping canvas after canvas
from their wooden stretchers.]

GREAVES
You'll see what a fire I'll make you

TINNIE
STOP IT WALTER... IN THE NAME OF GOD STOP IT !!

GREAVES
Shush Tinnie... it's all right..I'll not burn no pictures...just the wooden stretchers
Look there's quite a little pile and dry as tinder they are....................
Mmmm..get closer...feel that in your bones

TINNIE
Awww... this is...awww

GREAVES
Mmmm

TINNIE
Oh God ! Say someone wanted to buy one of your....

GREAVES
There's no sale for my oils...never was really

TINNIE
It's the end then

Nothing left to sell

GREAVES
I'll think of something

TINNIE
....
Walter... what about Whistler's letters ?

GREAVES
Eh ?

TINNIE
Jimmy's letters.. They're in that box.. Would they be worth anything ?

GREAVES
Shouldn't think so

TINNIE
I mean he's quite famous now ain't he ?...let me see...
[TINNIE opens the box;
takes out the letters in several bundles .]
Lord !
Such memories !
Those nights !
The Thames...by boat...always by boat....
Forever pestering me to go to the Pleasure Gardens with him he was
You at the oars Walter...

GREAVES
He'd pick out the different bits of colour in the distant lights
Make me memorise them...

TINNIE
The lights made me dizzy...

GREAVES
And the shapes of the buildings...

TINNIE
And the music...

GREAVES
We'd close our eyes and recite it one for the other;
'The second house is higher than the first...the fourth higher than all the rest...
Then thee pub with the Dutch gables
The church spire is twice the height of the tallest house...'
All that kind of thing

TINNIE
Dancing...

GREAVES
Stay at it we would till we had it word perfect
Then home to bed and paint it from memory next morning...

TINNIE
Always dancing !

GREAVES
Whistler couldn't dance... not like us

TINNIE
He could with me... only with me !
He always said that
There was a special...bond

GREAVES
Tied us all in... that bond

TINNIE
You tried to look like him...copied his dress... his walk..
You still do ... in your own tin-pot way...my poor Walter

GREAVES
If I did... it meant you never lost him

TINNIE

....

A shadow

GREAVES

More than a shadow I dare say

TINNIE

Hah !

GREAVES

Well !

TINNIE

....

You've always been a good man

GREAVES

Easy it were for me to be good
Never had..y'know...passion

TINNIE

You had passion !

GREAVES

Only for the work... the river

TINNIE

Walter !

GREAVES

Don't !
That was all you Tinnie

TINNIE

Didn't know what it was all about till I hadn't the strength to take hold of it...

Let it all slip away...
Pretending I was something I never could be...

GREAVES
You were such a beauty

TINNIE
Inside as wild as...
I remember the feeling.... I have it right now !
....
A bitch in heat trying to get out of the yard...God forgive me

GREAVES
Easy Tinnie...easy now

TINNIE
Them days everything had to be held in... know what I mean ?...held in
....
I should have made him give me child
I'd have that now if nothing else

GREAVES
Don't

TINNIE
His jokes...that energy...little body more like a child's than a grown man's
Stinging tongue to hide the hurt of wasted longing...fear of giving
Lost him to a cow with money and position
....
Ah well.. It's all over and done with long since
Now Walter take these letters to Mrs Pennell and see if she'll buy them
And don't sell them under a pound

GREAVES
Aw !

TINNIE
They're worth that and more !

GREAVES
She'd take them but she'd never part with no money...

TINNIE
Walter if we don't eat we'll die
Ask Mrs Jones if she'll give a bit of credit on them

GREAVES
Some of these is very private...you don't want strangers reading these

TINNIE
God I'd do murder for a plate of bacon and cabbage

GREAVES
Tell you what... see them very private ones ?
I wouldn't show them to no one
But the others... I'll take them round to old Goldberg on the Fulham Road
Goldberg always done right by us

TINNIE
Do it now !
And I'll heat up this tea and have it nice and warm when you gets back
Walter... take them all !

GREAVES
Definitely not the private ones... I...

TINNIE
But likely they're the ones'd fetch the money

GREAVES
I can't do it !

TINNIE
Suit yourself then

Go now... don't put it off
If he gives you enough for a bit of bacon...
Me mouth is watering at th...
Go for God's sake !

GREAVES
I'm going
Now don't count on anything.... he may laugh at me
Don't get yourself all excited

TINNIE
I gave up getting excited thirty years back
Go now

[Exit GREAVES.
TINNIE reads from the 'private' letters.]

TINNIE
Oh Jimmy ! Jimmy !...................
' Tinnie my jewel
My new picture, *At The Piano* is a triumph !
Now I am the pride of one end of Cheyne Walk as you are the pride of the other
Come dancing with me tonight in The Pleasure Gardens !
With you in my arms I promise you this
Together we shall defy gravity
And waltz through the stars into the Milky Way !...'

[In her phantasy TINNIE hears music and revelry
of earlier days...she waltzes through
space with the young artist.
GREAVES will enter the room and her phantasy,
breathless and triumphant, laden with food.]

GREAVES
Tinnie ! Food ! Eggs ! Bacon ! Cabbage !

TINNIE
Oh Jimmy dance with me again ! I'm so happy !

GREAVES
I'm so stiff ! Ha ha ha ha ! [THEY dance and sing]

BOTH [sing]
Tea butter and eggs
Bacon and cabbage and bread
Tea butter and eggs
It's the happiest day of my life !

TINNIE
God ! Mind the eggs !
[Laughing and breathless, THEY stop]

GREAVES
Look ! Money over !
Four pounds he gave me... four pounds for the letters

TINNIE
Oh Walter you are a marvel !

GREAVES
You won't believe this !
Goldberg is giving me another four pounds..sight unseen..for the old oils !

TINNIE
Aaagh ! We burned the stretchers !

GREAVES
He knows all that... I told him....he knows me and my work
Goldberg knows I do good work... I'm to bring them round

TINNIE
Well what are you waiting for ?
Here, we'll put them in these old sacks
Mind you bring them back... they're all I've got between me and the Winter's night
....
This one's me silken sheet... 'Best Milled flour'

And this here's me eiderdown quilt

...

Three pounds and four pounds... that's seven pounds
Oh my goodness ! Walter we best pay something off the rent eh ?

GREAVES

Yes...but not too much mind !

[THEY laugh happily.

Lights up on AUGUSTUS JOHN
and ELIZABETH PENNELL
in the Pennells' suite at the Savoy.]

JOHN

I knew Whistler only in his last years
A tired frail old shadow full of bitter memories

PENNELL

He simply could not forget or forgive injury

JOHN

I am blessed with the most wonderful memory
I can recall neither insult nor compliment beyond the half-hour

PENNELL

Whistler's compliments lasted longer than diamonds

JOHN

He came round to my studio in Fitzroy Street several times
No trouble feeding that fellow Elizabeth !
Pick...pick...never sat down... shoving his nose into everything...
Always on the move...pick... ate like an ailing sparrow
Maybe he had haemorrhoids

.....

Have you eaten all the sandwiches ?
You have an astonishing appetite, Lizzy !

PENNELL
You must read my book *In Defence Of Gluttony* Mr John

JOHN
Is that all I am to you : 'Mr John' ?
I devour everything I set my eyes on like a..a...

PENNELL
A lion

JOHN
Like a greedy old Welsh mountain goat ! Kiss me Lizzy !

PENNELL
I had better ask the maid to fetch more sandwiches

JOHN
If you do I shall ravish you both !

PENNELL
Augustus !
My husband will be back any minute

JOHN
Pennell is in a bawdy-house on the King's Road

PENNELL
Pennell is the staunchest Christian in London
...A most circumspect man.... very religious... like me... I am !

JOHN
Fair enough... all artists are religious...I worship Aphrodite... I'm a bloody religious maniac !

PENNELL
Idolater !

JOHN

I adore the female body

I must paint you Lizzy ! We'll have a child and I'll paint you with it on your arm

PENNELL

Child indeed !

JOHN

That's what God makes children for ! Whistler could have told you that ! Or Velásquez !

PENNELL

Have some tea

JOHN

I'll paint you as a tinker-woman... in the pose of a Renaissance angel... a muse..
About to take flight out over the sea...across the Isle of Dogs...
You'll sell milk-cans to unsuspecting sailors' wives on the quay at Greenwich ! Come !

[JOHN will tell his lie with conviction.]

This is work...nothing else
Throw the weight of your body on to that leg..mmm...so we get
The wonderful contours in the thrust of your...hip..

[JOHN is down on one knee as a knock is heard on the door.]

PENNELL

My husband ! Oh God !

[Exit JOHN in haste in other direction as Mrs PENNELL goes to the door. SHE returns to find him gone.]

PENNELL

Ah well !

....

What a heavenly day ! The first day I've really felt the winter is over

Mmmm the Thames...my Thames now !
I am the inheritor of Whistler's river as I am the guardian of his memory !
I'd give my right arm to have been in old Greaves's shoes
Working night after romantic night with the young Whistler
What a book I should have written !
Rowing over there to Battersea... up Chelsea Reach...The Pleasure Gardens at Cremorne !
Must telephone Heinemann about these mysterious Whistler pictures
Suddenly appearing out of nowhere
I mean I am supposed to be the authority on these things
They simply cannot be genuine..
Of course I know they can
It makes me look pretty damn silly...dozens of them !
I wonder did he lie to me... he had a strange sense of humour
What's that dealer's name ? Spencer
This can hit my fifth edition right where it hurts !
So I go out there and meet it coming ! Yankee style..cash in my fist !

[PENNELL walking towards Spencer's bookshop]

If there's another one of whistler's mother... My God !

.....

Music ? Back towards the river...

[PENNELL knocking at Spencer's closed door.]

Bookstore ! More like a privvy ! Can't see a thing through this filth...
What a slum !

[More loud knocking. SPENCER peers out.]

SPENCER
Did you say 'slum' ?

PENNELL
Elizabeth Pennell. I've written the new book on Whistler... the painter you know ?

SPENCER
Don't stock new books [Disappears.]

PENNELL
Sow ! [Louder knocking.]

SPENCER
Really !
I said I don't stock new books

PENNELL
I'd like to speak with you

SPENCER
....

PENNELL
A private word...

SPENCER
....

PENNELL
Shall I come right inside ?

SPENCER
.....

PENNELL
Please open up your store
.....
It's quite important
Something really big
Involving quite a heap of dough
I pay by cheque or cash on the nail
In dollars or in gold
....
Please will you open up your store ?

SPENCER
No

PENNELL
Oh !
You are in business, aren't you Mz Spencer ? I mean..

SPENCER
There's a lot of valuable antiquarian books in here
I don't let every Tom Dick and Harry into my shop Mrs Pennell
One simply must draw the line somewhere

PENNELL
I am American

SPENCER
Life is so short [Shuts door]

PENNELL
Well that's damned English insolence for you 1

[Exit PENNELL.
SPENCER is writing a letter.]

SPENCER
Ah...... 'William Marchant Esquire, Director, The Goupil Gallery, New Bond Street...
Dear William, Perhaps you would drop in to see me one of these fine Spring mornings. I have some pictures which may interest you.....'

[MARCHANT approaching.
He takes up the text of the letter...]

MARCHANT
' ...I am led to believe that there may be some connection between these pictures and your late friend Mr Whistler...but such matters you will be far better able to judge than could an old bookworm like me...'
Hmm... Now what the devil can Spencer be up to this time?

[A warm welcome.]

SPENCER
Ahh.. Nice to see you love !

MARCHANT
I came as soon as I got your note Sarah
How are you ?
[A cuckoo clock strikes.]

SPENCER
Come in come in William...this way... The place is a shambles as usual
Mind that lot in particular...very rare

MARCHANT
Sometimes I think you slipped out of a Dickens novel
Why do you pretend to be eccentric?

SPENCER
Ha ha ha ! Cup of tea ?

MAARCHANT
Ahh that would be wonderful Sarah !
Drank a lot of abominable wine down the King's Road last night

SPENCER
Now you take a look at that little treasure trove while I get the...
Milk or lemon ? I've no milk

MARCHANT
Lemon please...if you have it

SPENCER
I haven't. Ha ha ha !
[SHE will forget about the tea]

MARCHANT
All these canvasses is it ?
How extraordinary !

SPENCER
Yes and a number of etchings...sixty or seventy in all

MARCHANT
What a state ! Must have been dumped in a pig-sty...pooh !
[MARCHANT busy sorting through the canvasses.]

SPENCER
Old Goldberg on the Fulham Road brought them in... just as you see 'em...
Take your time now...D'you need a lamp William ?

MARCHANT
No it's fine

SPENCER
What d'you say ? Are they Whistlers ?

MARCHANT
Nothing yet by Whistler himself... but there is some...connection...yes...

SPENCER
A number of letters were found with them... all signed by Whistler
Quite genuine
They've been sold on... but I could still get my hands on them if...

MARCHANT
Anyone can see Whistler influenced many of these
That *Battersea Bridge By Moonlight*
But there's something else... something far more... primitive...
Quite fascinating ! Look at this ! Owes nothing to Whistler at all does it ?

SPENCER
I wouldn't really know to be quite honest

MARCHANT
Well you can see how naïve the concept, but the composition..superb !
You know Rousseau's work ?

SPENCER
You sure they're not Whistlers ?

MARCHANT
Absolutely

SPENCER
Hell !

MARCHANT
Entirely without sophistication...except where they obviously draw on Whistler
That's the puzzle... and such a sense of place: d'you see ?
The little boats painted as if each were known like you'd know the face of an old friend
Phew !... such dirt !
.... A signature here ! 'Greaves' 'W.Greaves'
'W' must be William... William Greaves
Never heard of him

SPENCER
You disappoint me William
I was full sure we were about to make our fortunes with half a hundred Whistlers !

MARCHANT
Not this time my darling

SPENCER
My father was Walter.. It could be 'W' for Walter

MARCHANT
Walter Greaves ?
......
Yes ! That's it ! Whistler's old assistant !
I never knew Greaves could paint like this !
When did he die ?

SPENCER
Never heard of him

MARCHANT
They had the boatyard at the end of Cheyne Walk

SPENCER
Oh I remember that ! Greaves's Boat Yard yes

MARCHANT
He had a pretty sister
Strange how one loses touch......My God !

SPENCER
Eh ?

MARCHANT
Like seeing a ghost !

SPENCER
You all right dear ?

MARCHANT
This is a painting of Whistler's funeral
I actually saw Greaves painting this

SPENCER
Back in the nineties

MARCHANT
No... Just seven or eight years ago
See the deserted street ? Nobody turned up to Whistler's funeral except a few staunch friends

SPENCER
I have his funny little book somewhere... *The Gentle Art Of Making Enemies*

MARCHANT

And there across the street in the drizzling rain
I saw his loyal rejected old comrade Greaves painting the scene..huh..for posterity
And dressed for all the world like a pathetic caricature of the Master

SPENCER

That pose of proud distain...coat of perfect cut...
One raven lock flying wild...flamboyant tie and cane..

MARCHANT

But Greaves's clothes were threadbare and green with age
His grey hair dyed with cheap shoe-black
And now in the rain the dye runs down his face and neck like dark surreal tears

SPENCER

Sad when a man must mirror another
Though we all wear masks William
Wilde used to say the mask tells us more than the mere face

MARCHANT

Whistler's sheer vitality soaked up all the energy about him
Left people without thought or feeling of their own
....
Well now am I to buy these off you or... ?

SPENCER

If they interest you... I paid Goldberg his price... I knew they had quality
Three hundred for the lot

MARCHANT

You are joking Sarah
Tch ! It'll cost a small fortune to tart up this mess into something presentable
Two

SPENCER
Two seventy-five... not a penny less !

MARCHANT
Impossible !

[SPENCER packing them away]

I tell you what I'll do... two-fifty and that's it ! Two-fifty !

SPENCER
I'll take two-fifty and the pick of the bunch when you have them framed

MARCHANT
No

SPENCER
Y'see ! You know they're a little gold-mine !
Two-seventy-five
Have we a deal ?

MARCHANT
You are a hard woman, Sarah
Two-seventy-five

SPENCER
Guineas is it ?

MARCHANT
Pounds Spencer pounds
Rascal !

[MARCHANT leaving Spencer's shop.]

Goldberg on the Fulham Road you say ?

[MARCHANT leaving Goldberg's shop *en route* to see Greaves JENNY shows the way.]

JENNY
Wasting your precious time going up there mister
Mr Goldberg bought the lot outa the goodness of his heart...pure charity

MARCHANT
Thank you..eh...Miss.... up th....?

JENNY
Nice people the Greaveses...very polite
Good family business they had down there in the boatyard
Never looked after it... see em now eh ?

MARCHANT
Is it...?

JENNY
Second house past the barrow
Nice people...tell em Jenny was askin for them

MARCHANT
Thank you so much... thank you...

[GREAVES and TINNIE content
over the embers of their fire
TINNIE answers MARCHANT'S knock.]

TINNIE
Walter...you 'ave a gentleman...

MARCHANT
Mr Greaves ! I thought you were d...
I'm so glad to see you

TINNIE
This 'ere is...oh dear I've forgotten your name already

MARCHANT
Marchant... William Marchant of the Goupil Gallery

We met many years ago Mr Greaves... and I believe we met too...Miss Greaves is it not ?

TINNIE

Miss Tinnie Greaves yes

MARCHANT

Of course ! You were Tinnie !

TINNIE

Still am...Tinnie

Me real name is Alice... but I don't recall nobody never calling me Alice

Always Tinnie it was... so that'll do me now for the rest of me days...

GREAVES

The Goupil ! My goodness ! Some wonderful shows there in the old days !

Yes... I remember you Mr Marchant... I remember you.... just as you are now

You must have been only a boy...

MARCHANT

My father sent me out into the world rather young I dare say

GREAVES

Sit down sit down... if you don't mind sitting on a tin box

Afraid you'll just have to take us as you finds us Mr Marchant

The years....

TINNIE

You'll 'ave a drop of tea... I'll warm it up for you

MARCHANT

No no I'm staying only a moment

I tell you frankly I had no idea if you were still... hale and hearty or...I mean...

GREAVES

You remembered us from the old days...that's good that's good

I expect you'll be writing a book about Whistler...

MARCHANT
I shall tell you all in just a moment
First I wanted to make contact again

GREAVES
We never managed to keep up with our old friends
I don't know...the years just...

MARCHANT
I may have a little business to discuss...
It's so good to see... both of you...fit and well !

GREAVES
I walk to Chelsea every day... there and back
It's where I like to work y' see

MARCHANT
Still working away ?

GREAVES
As best I can yes
They're not interested in my stuff these days

TINNIE
Never were

GREAVES
Still we survived

TINNIE
Hmmf ! Shoulda stuck to his trade... boat-buildin' with 'is father !

GREAVES
The river was there... somehow it made you want to paint it

MARCHANT
Even before Whistler came ?

GREAVES

Oh dear yes

Me an' 'Enry the brother.. We always painted

....

Of course we lost our heads over Jimmy Whistler...such a strong character I always says

Showed us how to use colour...how to paint really

Paint so thin... no detail...just the feeling...the impression

MARCHANT

Ah ! You changed your simple style to please him...what a pity

GREAVES

He wouldn't have us paint...only his way

Sometimes the longing for the old way of working'd come back...

Heh...he'd get home from Paris or somewhere and complain something terrible

Say we'd gone back to painting like savages... like cavemen he'd say

MARCHANT

There's quite a lot to be said for painting like cavemen... isn't there Miss Greaves ?

TINNIE

Quite a lot to be said for building boats if you ask me !

GREAVES

Mine would be the general composition

The brother...'Enry... loved to come along then and paint in every little detail

Every brick every pane of glass every board in the hull of a little boat

He'd paint in the nailheads if you let him ...heh heh !

Whistler had contempt for detail

Never would remember days or dates or anything 'superfluous to his art'

I never forgot that word of his...'superfluous'

TINNIE
Superfluous with selfishness he was
Take take take from all of us
When he got in with Society he wouldn't walk the same side of the street as poor Walter 'ere
Not to mention others he owed as much or more to
How can a man change like that ?

GREAVES
He was a bit naughty

TINNIE
Threw us away like old boots

GREAVES
It was that exhibition of his

MARCHANT
At the Goupil ?

GREAVES
I don't rightly recall
Some exhibition of his Tinnie and me never got to see
Near went berserk he did

TINNIE
Only waiting for a chance to ditch us

GREAVES
Cor ! Asked me very quiet-like did we see his exhibition
He knew well
'No I'm afraid we didn't' says I
'HA!!' He screams
'Jimmy' says I ' we didn't mean anything by it '
'HA HA !' says he 'didn't mean anything you wretched fellow ?
If you had meant anything perhaps I could forgive you !'
Turned on his heel then he did
And never spoke a civil word to me....to the day he died

....

TINNIE

Poor Walter ! Followed him around for thirty year
Never so much as a nod from Jimmy Whistler
You should have had more pride

MARCHANT

Well... we must continue this little chat very soon
Eh.....
My dear friends... forgive me...I... I am distressed to find...
You seem to lack the very basic comforts...eh....

TINNIE

Things ain't so bad now

GREAVES

We sold a lot of old canvasses the other day
Bit of a windfall... three pounds

MARCHANT

Three p... ?

TINNIE

Saved our precious life if the truth was told

MARCHANT

Eh... you might help me out in something...
I have all this furniture... quite serviceable... from my parents' place
And I have nowhere to put it
Beds chairs all kinds of things
I mean could I send some of it round to y...?

TINNIE

That's real kind of you Mr Marchant... real kind
But we wouldn't want to put nobody to no trouble over us
We manage...in our own..in our own little way

MARCHANT

But please ! You really would be doing me a favour

TINNIE
Well you put it like that...
No use pretendin' we don't need things
Lord ! It would be nice to sleep in a bed again !
Just that we learned to do without... you know what I mean ?

MARCHANT
First thing in the morning then
I'm not sure.. You may have to turn up the curtains

TINNIE
Oh I'd like that... turning up curtains !

MARCHANT
Oh and Mr Greaves... one other favour
Some day you have an hour or two to spare... if I called round for you in a cab
Would you come to the Goupil
And give me your opinion on some paintings I've come by ?
I've just had them restored and cleaned
And I have them hanging in their pristine glory !

GREAVES
Well I'd love to of course
Always liked the Goupil
And no need to bother about a cab for me
I'm well used to hoofing it around London

MARCHANT
I'll call
Needless to say I'll pay you a fee for your professional opinion

GREAVES
Heh heh ! Professional opinion
My opinion won't cost you nothing... heh heh!
I never got paid for giving my opinion these sixty years
I ain't expecting to start now ! Heh heh !
Any day you say...I'll be there

[MARCHANT leaving.]

MARCHANT

Monday ? Say I call for you around ten or a quarter past ....

GREAVES

Monday would be perfect

TINNIE

Ohh ! Turnin up curtains !

[LIGHTS down on TINNIE.
LIGHTS up on Goupil Gallery.]

MARCHANT

Now...after you Mr Greaves

GREAVES

The Goupil Gallery !
Whistler brought me here...quite recent

MARCHANT

It was a long time ago...
You must prepare yourself for... *VOILÁ* !
What about that Walter Greaves ?

[MARCHANT throws open the doors
of the main gallery where GREAVES can see
the painting which are his life's work
hung in style... cleaned restored and beautifully framed.
HE is overwhelmed.]

GREAVES

Oh..............oh...............OH !
I can't believe it !
My Resurrection !
....
But...why mine ?
....
Am I imagining ?

Oh dear me ...

MARCHANT
You recognise them ?

GREAVES
No.....Oh yes

MARCHANT
All of them ?.... Yours ?

GREAVES
Oh yes... oh yes
May I sit down please ?

MARCHANT
Forgive me... there
Now I'm going to have a drop of sherry... will you join me, Walter ?

GREAVES
That would be nice

MARCHANT
...
Not too dry I hope...

GREAVES
Your good heath Mr Marchant

MARCHANT
And yours !
Quite a surprise eh ?

GREAVES
A surprise ? Oh yes a surprise to say the least
....
And such beautiful frames

MARCHANT
They deserve it

GREAVES
So it was you bought them off Goldberg !
I can't say how pleased I am... so pleased

MARCHANT
Walter...I'd like to put on an exhibition of your work...
With your permission...here in my gallery
In my opinion you are quite an important artist

GREAVES
Oh my goodness ! Fancy that ! An exhibition !
Just about ready to meet my maker and you talk about an exhibition !
Heh heh heh !
Fancy that eh ! Will it be in the newspapers ?

MARCHANT
I should rather think so my dear Greaves
And you shall have a little commission on every picture sold

GREAVES
No not at all...I've been paid...Goldberg paid
They're all yours now...I want no commission

MARCHANT
You shall have it just the same

GREAVES
Heh heh... y'know Whistler..he'd always say his pictures remained his
No matter who bought them or how much they paid..heh!
'They're only on loan to the purchasers' he'd say

MARCHANT
He had a point

GREAVES
Well it's one point on which Greaves does not follow the Master

To be here...with all my work about me
In your wonderful gallery Mr Marchant.... it's like...

MARCHANT
Perhaps some time... if you can recall when you painted the different pictures...eh..
It would lend an added interest don't you think ?

GREAVES
I'll do it now !

MARCHANT
No ! Please !
I'll give you a list...come in at your leisure... tomorrow would do...
And jot down the days and dates and whatever comes into your head about them
We might include it as a Preface to the catalogue...
Today let's just enjoy them !
Next week...THE GRAND GREAVES EXHIBITION !!

INTERVAL

PART TWO

[PENNELL speaking on the telephone
from the Savoy.
MARCHANT and GREAVES wait at the Goupil Gallery
for the expected throng, which does not materialise.]

PENNELL
The Goupil ?
I have no intention of being seen there Sir Henry
.....
A genius ? Walter Greaves a genius ? Ha ha ha !
He was a boatman on the Battersea ferry !
Whistler used him as a kind of footman... a message boy...
I shouldn't waste my time or money if I were you dear
No one of the slightest importance is going
....
Yes... ha ha ha ha ! Exactly !
Marchant has made a serious mistake getting involved with this class of person
The kindest thing is simply to stay away

MARCHANT
Something very strange is going on here Walter...

PENNELL
A rather dodgy bookseller first tried to pass them off as being genuine...y'know... Whistlers
I had to go down there and make it quite clear I'd stand for no skullduggery !
....
Ha ha ha ha ha ha !

[BLACKOUT on PENNELL .]

MARCHANT
My exhibitions are always packed to the doors

GREAVES
There's several people gone in

MARCHANT
I expected a couple of hundred

[AUGUSTUS JOHN has been seeing the exhibition.]

JOHN
Hey there !

MARCHANT
Augustus ! Good to see you
You know Walter Greaves

JOHN
To my shame I didn't until today !
Greaves that *Race Day On Hammersmith Bridge*... the most stunning thing I've seen since...
I swear to God ! Who taught you to paint like that ?
Not Whistler for sure... your style goes back to something very old...
Do you know what I mean William ?

MARCHANT
I said it... Rousseau

JOHN
Bloody Botticelli man !

GREAVES
That *Race Day*.. Is really my old way of working...
I was only a boy...sixteen or seventeen... when I painted that

JOHN
No training ?

GREAVES
Afraid not

JOHN
Christ you lucky dog!
I've spent ten years trying to unlearn all the shit they stuffed into me at the Slade

GREAVES
There was always someone painting on the river in them days..

JOHN
At last I'm beginning to see what colour is about....

GREAVES
Turner lived right by us...

JOHN
Maybe now I can start to paint !

GREAVES
My dad used to row him about all hours of the day and night
My dad thought Turner was a retired sea-captain
Hankering for the sea when the moon was up
But he'd put out on the river sometimes at two or three in the morning....
A bit like I done later for Whistler
.....
Me and my brother used to decorate all the boats on Chelsea Reach...
That's how we got the feeling for paint

JOHN
Oh God y'hear that Marchant ?
Like the great gypsy artists painting their caravans
Right back to the roots of Art....Religion...Magic !
Hug me Greaves ! Mmmmh ! Magic !
Be back in tomorrow for another look !

[JOHN rushes out to meet the entering PENNELL]

GREAVES
My goodness... what a whirlwind !

MARCHANT
A good eye and a good heart
But where are all my clients ?

GREAVES
Is that a newspaperman ?

MARCHANT
A very important one... Clutton-Brock of *The Times*

[Lights down on GREAVES and MARCHANT .
JOHN embraces PENNELL kissing her hungrily.]

JOHN
Where have you been you devil ?

PENNELL
Oh !
My husband is parking the automobile
We lost our chauffeur

JOHN
My God ! I'll help you look for him !

PENNELL
Silly !

JOHN
Lizzy I must see you !
I'm nursing my virginity to the point of distraction ! Come !

PENNELL
I can't !

JOHN
You're coming to Dorset with me !
I've leased this mad fairyland of wild woods and little dales
Secret gardens where we can lie naked all day long !

We live like gypsies there !
Write to your husband on the train...

PENNELL
I understand you already have two wives... and I dread to think how many children...
Down in your Fairyland !
Go there and be happy in your savagery..

JOHN
You are my only true tinkerwoman !

PENNELL
We are dining with The Ambassador

JOHN
The devil take your Ambassador !

PENNELL
Come to my Thursday *soirée* !

JOHN
We'll not waste another night with that gang of frauds

PENNELL
Everyone will be there... Orpen... Sickert...
You need the company of artists tha...

JOHN
I need a fuck...

PENNELL
Don't use that language to me

JOHN
And it's your bounden duty to give it to me

PENNELL
You said you simply wanted to paint me

JOHN
Simply ? There's nothing simple about painting a bloody portr...

PENNELL
Tch !

JOHN
..ait ! Throw away your shoes and we'll hike barefoot out of London and...

PENNELL
You're crazy !

JOHN
...We'll tinker through Devonshire Cornwall and Dorsetshire
Hugging the ditches of primrose and hay...

PENNELL
We're expected at The Embassy at seven...

JOHN
Bully o'er Bodwin Moor, Exmoor and Dartmoor
Windswept we'll lie in a hollow of green..

PENNELL
Breathless I'm feeling your rising to lie on me...

JOHN
Gypsy by Bridport by Falmouth and Perranport
The salt in your mouth in your nose in your eyes...

PENNELL
We were to dine *al fresco...*

JOHN
Sleeping on sandhills feeding on sea-cockles
Ride as the waves ride the thundering sea...

PENNELL
Oh Augustus !

JOHN
Well I can't paint you without making love with you... you know that
Still you torture me with your New England prudery

PENNELL
Pennsylvania

JOHN
Pennsylvanian prudery

PENNELL
Now... Marchant will never forgive me if I don't give him my opinion on his exhibition !
Ha ha ha ha !
Do come on Thursday Mr John !
Come early and we can discuss our elopement ! Ha ha !

JOHN
I'll come on Wednesday Mrs Pennell
Then we'll have plenty of time for our discussion

[Lights up on GREAVES and MARCHANT .]

GREAVES
Oh dear... that critic...is he angry ?

MARCHANT
He'll never speak to anyone till he has his piece written

PENNELL
Thursday...at six
At least the sandwiches will still be fresh

JOHN
At least the sandwiches

[After a furtive glance up and
down the street outside exit JOHN.
PENNELL enters the exhibition.]

GREAVES
Quite cross-looking I should say

MARCHANT
He came to see for himself
I'm grateful for that
And look... here's Mrs Pennell
Come and meet her... she's written Whistler's biography

GREAVES
You speak to her Mr Marchant
I've seen quite a lot of her recently

MARCHANT
Eh ? Oh....excuse me a moment
Mrs Pennell ! Delighted you could come ! Enjoying the show ?

PENNELL
Immensely ! It's.....
Ha ha ha ! Perfectly hilarious !

MARCHANT
Pardon ?

PENNELL
It's a joke is it not ?
The best of these are not by Greaves

MARCHANT
Wha...?

PENNELL
Jimmy probably threw that one in the dustbin !
Greaves picked it up...stuck his name and a date on it... hah

MARCHANT
Well Whistler never painted this !

PENNELL
I wouldn't argue with you there
.....
And this ? *A Nocturne In Grey And Blue* of 1862 ?

MARCHANT
Why not ?

PENNELL
Because Whistler invented that style ten years later !
Are you telling me Greaves painted like that even before he met Whistler ?

MARCHANT
Mr Greaves has dated all these pictures himself... would you lik...?

PENNELL
The man is little better than a tramp
Whistler would cross the street to avoid the fellow
As I do now

MARCHANT
But your book.... quotes Greaves extensively... praises his keen memory...

PENNELL
I shall correct that in the next edition I assure you !
Good day to you sir !
Marchant you really should have consulted the experts
Before engaging on an adventure like this !
[Exit PENNELL]

MARCHANT
I'm afraid our friend has been saying rather nasty things about us...

GREAVES
But why ? I've always helped her any way I could

MARCHANT
You threaten her god
She is the keeper of the shrine

GREAVES
I loved Jimmy from the first day I met him
I'd help keep his shrine

MARCHANT
She won't have that
....
Ah well I suppose we may close up shop
I'm so disappointed for you

GREAVES
Oh I'm more than satisfied
You've lost a great deal of money haven't you ?

MARCHANT
It isn't the money !
My clients should have come to judge for themselves !

GREAVES
These pictures of mine... they're all good work
They'll sell all right

MARCHANT
I can't sell if they don't even come in to look !
....
You know... I did sell a few engravings....
Here... I'll give you a little commission on account... five pounds all right ?

GREAVES
No no no...

MARCHANT

I insist ! Take it !
Now I'll find you a cab and we'll get a good night's sleep if nothing else

[Exeunt.
JENNY nearby watching
the passing of the night.]

JENNY

The river through the city
The longing in the gut
Ten million hungry faces
Waiting all their life
For the right time
For the right this
For the right that
For the jewel in the mud
Of the river through my city
The longing in the gut
Ten million hungry faces
Waiting all their life
For nothing !

[Morning.
Newsvendor's cry heard as
MARCHANT walks down New Bond Street
to his gallery. JENNY selling papers.]

JENNY

Times Mr Marchant ?

MARCHANT

Please

[MARCHANT will search for
a review of his exhibition on the usual page.]

JENNY

And a penny change guv

MARCHANT
HELL ! Not even a mention !

JENNY
Hear as how you've got yourself all over the Leader Page, Mr Marchant

MARCHANT
Wha... ? What ?
GOOD GOD ALMIGHTY 1

JENNY
AN UNKNOWN MASTER !
EXHIBITION OF AN UNKNOWN MASTER AT THE GOUPIL GALLERY !

MARCHANT
How extraordinary !

JENNY
THE ROYAL ACADEMY SHOULD NOW MAKE SOME REPARATION FOR THE LONG PUBLIC NEGLECT OF THIS MASTER...WALTER GREAVES ON WHOSE DISCOVERY MR MARCHANT IS TO BE CONGRATULATED 1

MARCHANT
YIPPIE !! I've done it ! I've done it !!

[THE CAST gathers on stage as CLIENTS who plunge into panic-buying of Greaves's work vying with each other for the best pictures, waving cheques and bundles of cash.]

CAST [in hubbub]
I must have number twenty-two [etc etc.]

MARCHANT
I'm doing everything I can !

A CLIENT
I've got the dough and mean to buy

A CLIENT
Four hundred pounds for sixty-four !

A CLIENT
I have to buy or die !

MARCHANT
Sixty-four is sold !

A CLIENT
Twenty-three is mine ! [etc etc]

CAST
We've got the dough and mean to buy !
EVERYTHING !

MARCHANT
One at a time ! Please !

CLIENT
Just charge this picture up to me !

MARCHANT
Plaisir and thank you Lady B. !

CLIENT
Five hundred pounds for sixty-five !

MARCHANT
I'll send the bill m' Lord
.....
Of course a cheque will do !

CAST
We've got the dough and mean to buy !
EVERYTHING !!!

[AUGUSTUS JOHN bottle of Champagne in hand calls cheerfully.]

JOHN
Hey William ! What hit this place overnight ?
You struck gold again man !

MARCHANT
Something like that
Oh Augustus give Walter a hand with those Press people will you ?

JOHN
Delighted Willie-bach
'Way there ! Give that man half a chance and we'll answer all the questions you like !

[CAST metamorphosise into PRESS CORPS who engage in their own HUBBUB.]

ALL
Did Whistler teach you how to paint ? [etc etc.]

REPORTER
How many children have you sir ?

REPORTER
Did you know Mr Oscar Wilde ?

ALL
Tell everything... we need to know EVERYTHING !

JOHN
ONE AT A TIME !
You sir !

REPORTER
Mr Greaves is it true to say you were painting night pieces on the Thames
Before you met Whistler ?

GREAVES

Oh yes...me an 'Enry me brother
We painted day and night pieces from when we was boys
Fifteen or younger

REPORTER

What school do you follow ? Impressionism ?

GREAVES

We never went to school after the Third Book

[Laughter.]

JOHN

Walter Greaves is that rarest phenomenon... and entirely unique artist
He would have painted just as he paints now
If there had never been another artist or school of painting in England
He is the perfect... naïve genius !
Yes my friend ?

REPORTER

The Times refers to you as 'The Unknown Master'
How have you managed to remain unknown all these years ?

GREAVES

Unknown Master ? Heh heh !
You ask any bloke around The King's Head And Eight Bells on the Embankment
They'll tell you I'm not unknown
Everyone in Chelsea knows Walter Greaves...

[PRESS titter.]

REPORTER

They say you've been selling your work along the Embankment
For as little as half a Crown
People are paying four and five hundred pounds here this morning and...

GREAVES

Well the watercolours is half a Crown...five for ten shillings
I never really sell the oils down there... people wouldn't have the money
Y'see oils is so dear...
I'd have to charge thirty shilling or even two pound for the oil paintings

REPORTER

Even after this ?

GREAVES

Oh yes... they're worth it
You can see I do good work

[Laughter.
Enter TINNIE .]

TINNIE

Yoohoo ! Yoohoo !

JOHN

Enough ! That will be all for this morning my friends

[PRESS drift away]

TINNIE

Walter !

GREAVES

There's me sister Tinnie... I'll go and talk to her

JOHN

You must introduce me

GREAVES

Well Tinnie ?

TINNIE

Aaay ! Fancy all this for our Walter !
My this really is something ain't it then ?

GREAVES
Eh... this here is Mr Augustus John
A very-well-thought-of young painter

JOHN
Very-badly-thought-of in some quarters I'm afraid Tinnie
I warn you... I have a terrible reputation with the ladies... terrible !

TINNIE
Ooooh ! Delighted I'm sure Mr John

JOHN
Gussy ! Mmmmm [Kisses her hand noisily.]

TINNIE
Ooeeooh! Don't know when an 'andsome young man kissed my 'and
You shan't have a terrible reputation with me....Gussy !
Whistler kissed me every time he seen me he did... Always kissin' me
one way or the other...
A proper caution he were... for kissin'

JOHN
The story of my life Tinnie !
"A proper caution for kissin' "
Champagne ?

TINNIE
Well Gussy... I don't mind if I do !
[TINNIE will throw back
the drink and the refill in a gulp.]
Agggggh ! That was good !
Champagne !

JOHN
Another ?

TINNIE
Why not ?
....

Oh this is the life !
......
You know... in Fulham...where me and Walter lives...
We 'ardly never 'as Champagne
.....
Since the old days... I think it would be no exaggeration to say
I 'ave been a stranger to Champagne
As to many other of the...eh...necessities of life ! Hic !
Especially I 'ave been a stranger to the attend...attentions
Of dashing young men the likes of you Gussy I think you're dangerous 'andsome !

JOHN
And I have been a stranger to delightful ladies the likes of you Tinnie!

TINNIE
Nonsense ! I'm old enough to be your grandmother !

JOHN
I was madly in love with my grandmother !

TINNIE
One thing I never would do... come between a man and his grandmother !
She might scratch me eyes out
I know I would if I had you if you were my age if you wanted me
God this Champagne makes me feel....... I believe I could fly !
I'd love to dance !
How can these people have all this Champagne and everything and not dance ?

[TINNIE can hear music.]

JOHN
May I have the next waltz m'dear ?

TINNIE
A pleasure..m'dear !

[TINNIE and JOHN lilt and waltz, whirling around until TINNIE'S wig falls off.]

TINNIE

Agh me wig ! Aah..ha ha ha !

[THEY stop, laughing and out of breath. They are in front of Whistler's portrait of Tinnie.]

Is it straight ?

JOHN

It's fine ! Ha ha ha ha !
Oh Tinnie look ! This portrait... you isn't it ?

TINNIE

Oooh can you believe I ever looked like that ?
I was a bit of a beauty

JOHN

You are
....
You know... this portrait of you Tinnie
May be Walter's greatest achievement
...Another dimension entirely... Nothing naïve about this !
Did Whistler see it ?

TINNIE

In a way

JOHN

In a way ?

TINNIE

Never would look at it
Got quite angry 'e did if I tried to talk about it
Reckon 'e thought our Walter was goin' a bit above 'imself
Paintin' grand portraits... even if it were only of poor Tinnie

JOHN

I can see why

TINNIE
Walter never meant to be cheeky to no one
Went to the other extreme if you ask me

JOHN
See this portrait ?   He achieved something here
That eluded Whistler all his days...

TINNIE
Fancy that !

JOHN
...A combination of...elegance...economy... perfect composition
And above all... that sureness of touch...
Brushstrokes like...caresses !
God! If only I could love things like Walter does
Without destroying everything I...

TINNIE
He loved me y'know... but he'd never marry me
Had to marry someone with a bit of money and... position
Very important it was for him to get in with the toffs

JOHN
If I ever marry again see
I'll marry a gypsy
Live in a painted caravan by the side of a ditch...

TINNIE
No

JOHN
No... on top of a hill looking out over
The sun-ripened moon-crazy thundering sea !

TINNIE
Oh Jesus !   If... if only...

[Light change. Exit TINNIE.
MARCHANT JOHN and GREAVES

at lunch with the Chelsea Arts Club.]

MARCHANT
...And so it is with the deepest pleasure that I present
Our distinguished guest Mr Walter Greaves with this very small cheque
As a token of our very great esteem
Walter... from the artists and art-lovers of The Chelsea Arts Club !
[Applause and acclaim.
MARCHANT hands over the cheque.]

VOICES
Speech ! Speech !
[GREAVES obliges.]

GREAVES
Eh... I'm not sure I ever had a cheque before... [Ripple of laughter from CAST.]
I haven't never been a member of your club much as I would like to have...eh...been
I couldn't afford the subscription even if you had invited me to join
[Murmurs from CAST.]
Maybe now with this cheque I can become a member...
[Laughter and applause.]

VOICE
Here here !

GREAVES
You know I was nearly guest of honour at a banquet here...oh thirty years back ?
[Aside to JOHN] Is it all right to say this ?

JOHN
Say anything you want !
[GREAVES warms to his subject.]

GREAVES
Well y'see Whistler had sort-of rejected me and my family

I was more than upset... used to hang about places as I might run into him
Hoping for the miracle...the friendship like the old days
You may have noticed I dress a bit like him an' all...
[CAST sniggers]
So this night I knew your club was giving a banquet in honour of Whistler
Foolish as I was in them days... about the time things was ready to start
There was me hangin' around the lobby... not invited nor nothing of course
Just hoping Jimmy would see me going in
The old toffs from the Committee [Laughter] Heh
These toffs take me to be Whistler !
Fusses me up here and starts
Pouring Champagne and everything into me at a great rate
And us all talking and nodding and chatting about art
And my work and Chelsea... you can imagine
Suddenly that door bursts open and in storms whistler bristling like a tomcat !
Stops six inches from my face... screws in his monocle
Like he was seeing himself in a dirty mirror...know what I mean ?
Not a sign of recognition like I wasn't there
Walks through me and takes over the whole show
For the rest of the night !
......
They didn't throw me out mind
Put me sitting way over there well away from the toffs
Gave me dinner with the rest... wonderful meal !
Though if you ask me the food has improved here if anything !
[Laughter and applause
MARCHANT and JOHN in conversation
with GREAVES .]

JOHN

...What ? The Post-Impressionists ? I thought very little of them !

GREAVES

Mr John !

MARCHANT
I don't believe you !

JOHN
Oh yes very little...the first time
A fortnight later I was back
God ! I stood in front of that Van Gogh self-portrait for a solid hour...mesmerised !
It was their damned name had put me off the scent
'Post-Impressionists indeed !
THEY ARE BLOODY PRIMITIVES ! LIKE YOU GREAVES... PRIMITIVES !

GREAVES
Oh now now...

JOHN
I mean it... your *Race Day* could be painted from Gauguin's palette
And you have Van Gogh's sense of... of the unity of Creation !

GREAVES
How ever do they buy all those bright colours ?

JOHN
Champagne ?

GREAVES
Yellows and reds and greens... wonderful blues !
Mostly I use grey nowadays... it's priced very reasonable

JOHN
By Christ Greaves there's no shortage of bright colours about my studio !
Just you walk in and help yourself..d'you hear that now ?

GREAVES
You're a good man Mr John

JOHN
Drink up Walter-bach !

MARCHANT
I must tell you....the exhibition may well go to New York !
All the New York papers want to know about our new master !

GREAVES
Americans ! Fancy that !

JOHN
The only pity is you ever fell under Whistler's spell...
That stopped you in your tracks

GREAVES
He woke us from a deep sleep

JOHN
To dominate you !
You... painting your wonderful dreams...

GREAVES
It weren't like that... not really

JOHN
None of my business anyway... you probably wanted to be dominated
Shush ! I feel a Limerick coming on !

MARCHANT
Spare us !

GREAVES
Are you all right ?

JOHN
Hold it !
....
"To a primitive artist called Greaves
Who painted sweet river naïves

Said Whistler 'tis best
If your work is suppressed
So my own reputation succeeds !" Ha ha ha ha !

GREAVES
Oh dear oh dear ! He didn't suppress my work really
Just thought nothing of it like

JOHN
Ah Walter Greaves... I have lost my innocence !
I envy you

GREAVES
Mmm I been around
You'd be surprised Mr John

JOHN
NO ! ART IS INNOCENCE !
You shall be our high priest Walter !

GREAVES
Heh heh heh heh ! High priest eh ?
....
Mr Marchant I been thinking....eh...
Would it be very extravagant for me to start painting in oils again ?
The price of p....

MARCHANT
PAINT ? THE PRICE OF PAINT IS IT ?
Walter... paint another *Race Day* for my gallery and I'll buy you buckets of paint !
Rivers of bloomin paint ! Ha ha ha ha ! 'Paint !' Ha ha ha !

GREAVES
I like this

JOHN
See all this food lad ? A little s... ?

GREAVES

Oh thank you no... I've had quite a...sufficiency
Mr John... do you think I..... could I take a little something home to our Tinnie..she

JOHN

My God man... take all you can carry...I'll get a bag !

MARCHANT

I'll do it... *Garçon !*

VOICE [Off]

Oui monsieur ?

MARCHANT

Un sac s'il vous plait !... Un sac pour la chienne !

VOICE [Off]

Tout de suite Monsieur Marchant !

JOHN

Your glass !

GREAVES

I shall be tipsy if I do !

JOHN

Of course you shall ! Here !
MY FRIENDS...I DRINK TO GREAVES...THE UNKNOWN MASTER !

ALL

TO THE UNKNOWN MASTER !

[PENNELL angry at what she reads in the newspapers.]

PENNELL

Unknown master ! What damn rubbish !
These rags will print anything to make a sensation !

The Greaves thrash was selling as fast as they could rake in the money yesterday...
Over two thousand pounds in one day !
Just wait till I complete my research on Greaves and the dating of these pictures ...
Particularly that one they say was exhibited in the Great 1862 Exhibition ....

[Enter JOHN]

Oh it's you !
....
I never thought to see you take sides against me

JOHN
I couldn't be against you
Greaves has to be judged on his merits

PENNELL
He's an imposter and a liar !

JOHN
So am I

PENNELL
Tch !

JOHN
Hah..y'know Whistler once told me he left the United States
In despair of anything worthwhile happening in a country
Whose national hero couldn't tell a lie !

PENNELL
He'd have something to say about Greaves forging his Nocturnes
He'd punch him right on the nose !

JOHN
Did you see his *Race Day ?*

PENNELL
Daubings of an adolescent... a retarded adolescent

JOHN
Come with me to see it again

PENNELL
No...you're so...

JOHN
I didn't come here to talk about Greaves...

PENNELL
Loyalty is very important to me

JOHN
Now she hates me
Shall I go ?

PENNELL
No

JOHN
Oh Lizzy !

[Enter JENNY]

JENNY
Sorry mum... message for Mr John from Madame Strindberg
Oh Mr John... Madame killed herself again and ain't feeling at all well

PENNELL
Gracious ! I'll fetch my doctor !

JOHN
It's not a doctor she needs it's a good kick up the backside

JENNY
Oooh Mr John you are awful !

PENNELL
Is she really dead ?

JENNY
In her final throes mum
Says goodbye to me an' gives me a sovereign
Anyway I knew she was for killing herself when she sent me to make the Bovril

PENNELL
Bovril ?

JENNY
Madame favours washing down the poison with Bovril mum

JOHN
It would make an excellent advertisement
"Wash down your overdose with BOVRIL ! "

JENNY
Mr John always comes with me and the stomach-pump man

JOHN
Well he's not coming any more so get along with you !

PENNELL
I'm surprised at Madame Strindberg sending such a pretty girl to fetch Mr John...

JENNY
Thank you mum I'm sure...Mr John always knows exactly what to do

PENNELL
I never doubted him on that score child

JOHN
She has hounded me across six countries
She has hired an assassin to do me in !

JENNY

Madame says she killed herself 'cos he called her something terrible
To the editor of *The Illustrated London News* mum !

JOHN

Ha ha ha ! I called her 'The Walking Hell-bitch Of The Western World' Ha ha ha !
If the name sticks Synge will sue me for every penny I've got !

PENNELL

Poor woman !

JOHN

She drove Strindberg to a lunatic's grave
I owe her nothing

JENNY

No mum exceptin' she says Mr John took advantage of her first off...

JOHN

She climbed in my window and raped me where I lay sleeping like a babe !

JENNY

If she dies proper this time mum Mr John won't never forgive himself mum !

JOHN

Let her die and no great loss to anyone !

JENNY

Oooooooooh ! I'll be on the streets if she croaks it ! On the streets! Aaaaaagh !

JOHN

You'll come to Dorset with me if she does

JENNY
Wouldn't... take advantage would you sir ?

JOHN
Of course I would

JENNY
AAAAAGH !

PENNELL
I shall find you a position if anything happens
Come straight here...any hour of the day or night

JENNY
Thank you mum

JOHN
Thank you mum

PENNELL
Not you you rascal !

JOHN
Run off now and get your stomach-pump man

JENNY [*Cocquette*]
You be over in a bit to see everything's all right Mr John ?

JOHN
Ahem ! I'll send the doctor
I have important business to discus with eh Mrs Pennell's husband

JENNY
That stomach-pump man don't care much for women
Much obliged to you mum ! [Curtsey and exit]

JOHN
Where were we ?

PENNELL
Loyalty
You don't even love me

JOHN
I'm obsessed by you

PENNELL
There's a bit of me that doesn't really care

JOHN
My tinker-woman

PENNELL
Yes

JOHN
I saw her the first day...

PENNELL
Then there's the Quaker-girl who cares about everything

JOHN
I shall make love to each in turn !

PENNELL
No... you must never make love to the Quaker-girl
She'd be so ashamed
Only the tinker-woman
....
Come my pretty !

[BLACKOUT. Light change.
The Goupil. PENNELL hammering
on MARCHANT 's door.]

PENNELL
MARCHANT !

MARCHANT
Mrs Pennelll !? Good morning to you

PENNELL
Marchant I have the most disturbing and serious compliant to make
Concerning this...'exhibition' !

MARCHANT
Good heavens ! Would you like to talk in my office ?

PENNELL
What I got to say can be heard by the world !
BY THE WORLD !

MARCHANT
Ahem... of course

PENNELL
I stand over this as The Catalogue of the Great Exhibition of 1862 sir !
Can you say as much for the catalogue of this...charade ?

MARCHANT
Exhibition
I hope so

PENNELL
Does or does not your Catalogue say that Number 47 in this so-called exhibition
Was also shown at the Great Exhibition of 1862 ?

MARCHANT
Eh yes... It says that in Mr Greaves's letter to us... that is his Preface to the Catalogue

PENNELL
Well I say 'Mr' Walter Greaves is a liar !

MARCHANT
Mrs Pennell please guard your language !

PENNELL
Read that Catalogue sir and find if you can
Any mention good bad or indifferent
To you precious 'master' !
Greaves was as unknown then as he was last week
And will be next week except as an imposter a liar and a damned charlatan !

MARCHANT
Hmmmm... It certainly seems that Mr Greaves has made a mistake in the matter of da....

PENNELL
MISTAKE ! MISTAKE ? !
IT'S A DAMN MISREPRESENTATION SIR !!!
YOU HAVE BEEN TAKING THE PUBLIC'S MONEY ON FOOT OF A TISSUE OF LIES !

MARCHANT
Mr Greaves is a man of more than seventy
It's quite possible he's made a mistake over..

PENNELL
HA !!

MARCHANT
The quality of his work doesn't depend on dates...it has been acclaimed purely on its merits..

PENNELL
UNDER FALSE PRETENSES SIR !
UNDER FALSE PRETENSES !

MARCHANT
If you can discuss this in more temperate language I shall endeavour...
Look... I shall withdraw the entire preface !

And I shall personally investigate the matter quite thoroughly...

PENNELL
I should damn well think you will !

MARCHANT
Yes.... Now believe me... I am most grateful that you have brought this matter to my attention

PENNELL
HAH !

MARCHANT
Unfortunately I must go abroad in the morning...just for a week
...But you have my personal assurance on this...
Investigations will be initiated before I go
And I shall give it complete priority when I get back...

PENNELL
A week is a helluva long time
When London is hell-bent on canonising this...
This moth-eaten Puncinello of yours...
And damning the greatest artist of the nineteenth century ... James Whistler !

MARCHANT
I yield to no man.. Or woman ha ... in my admiration for Whistler !
As you know .. he had a long and fruitful association with us in this gallery
Why in this very room I mounted his... his triumph...heh..
His apotheosis he called it !

PENNELL
That's as may be...

MARCHANT
It's all in your own book Mrs Pennell
Is a week so long to wait ?

PENNELL
Oh...all right...I'll do nothing till you get back

MARCHANT
Good

PENNELL
But I shall expect a full and public resolution of this matter absolutely without delay !

MARCHANT
You have my word on it

PENNELL
One week !

[Exit MARCHANT .
MARCHANT 's week abroad passes.
PENNELL writing furiously to the newspapers as
MARCHANT returns to the anxiously waiting GREAVES .]

GREAVES
The newspapers been full of terrible things from Mrs Pennell...

MARCHANT
You should have nailed the first lie the moment it appeared !

GREAVES
I haven't the education for writing to the newspapers

MARCHANT
Mrs Pennell gave me her solemn word she'd do nothing till I got back

GREAVES
She can't take away all that's happened

MARCHANT
She can take away my reputation
The date on that moonlight scene is obviously wrong !
I'm just kicking myself I didn't see it sticking out like...

When did you paint it ?

GREAVES
No idea

MARCHANT
God !
And Number 47 ?   Mrs Pennell dug up the 1862 Catalogue
Of course it isn't in it
Nor was there anything else by you in the exhibition

GREAVES
There should have been

MARCHANT
For heaven's sake man !

GREAVES
Maybe there was a printer's error

MARCHANT
Now look... I must have the truth
Greaves... are any of these discarded Whistlers that you... finished off or something ?

GREAVES
I shouldn't think so

MARCHANT
You don't know ?
....
That moonlight scene looks suspiciously like a Whistler I saw back in...

GREAVES
Some of 'em I painted from Whistler's memory know what I mean ?
Ha ha !

MARCHANT
I don't see anything to laugh at

GREAVES
Well yes... I do believe that's one of them I painted from Jimmy's memory

MARCHANT
Oh God !

GREAVES
"The second house is higher than the first' says I
"THE FIRST IS HIGHER THAN THE SECOND ! " he screams
Insisted then I paint from his picture
His memory he says vastly improves on mere nature Ha ha!

MARCHANT
Are you telling me this is just a copy of a Whistler ?

GREAVES
No... just painted from his memory

MARCHANT
I believed every word you told me...days dates...

GREAVES
"The date on a picture is purely the business of the artist" he'd say
"It bears no relations to clocks or calendars "

MARCHANT
You're no Whistler Greaves... you can't afford that kind of sophistry

GREAVES
I don't know what that means... 'sophistry'
The Times says I'm the new master

MARCHANT
At sixteen you had the makings of an important naïve artist

You threw that away when you became his... whatever you were to him...

GREAVES
I threw nothing away Mr Marchant

MARCHANT
It's time you faced up to reality

GREAVES
We were the closest friends imaginable

MARCHANT
You botched up your friendship like you botched up everything else in your life...
Including what might have been the sale of the century here !
For a week I had London eating out of that [hand] !

GREAVES
I always said it was good work

MARCHANT
Marketing. ..good marketing man !
That's the new art of the twentieth century...that's my art...marketing art
With a reputation carefully build up over a lifetime
I could stick toilet-paper into fancy frames and sell it here at a hundred pounds a time !
You messing about with dates has put all that at risk
There's always a Greaves or a Pennell... or a Whistler to pull me back...
....
Like the river through my city the longing in my gut
Past ten million hungry faces
I've waited all my life for the right art at the right time
For the jewel in the music of the river through my city
I waited all my life to get everything... right... just once !
....
Now look here Greaves...if you have the slightest shadow of a doubt

Of there being so much as brushstroke of Whistler's on any picture in this exhibition
For god's sake let us get it off the wall right now !

GREAVES
They're all one hundred *per cent* mine

MARCHANT
Good.... now....

GREAVES
Except for that business of painting from Jimmy's memory

MARCHANT
DON'T LET ME HEAR ONE MORE WORD ABOUT JIMMY'S MEMORY OR I SHALL EXPLODE !
Forget Jimmy's memory or you and I will be the laughing-stock of London !
If you can swear to me you painted every last one of them
I'll fight Pennell on authorship and quality and save what I can
From this debacle you've landed me in
Now I must get on with my business...[Reads newspaper]
.....
Oh my God ! The tramp !

GREAVES
Marketing... ?
Marketing I venture to say Mr Marchant... is a superfluous activity

[MARCHANT and PENNELL
at war through the newspapers]

MARCHANT
The slag has stabbed me in the back !

PENNELL
Why keep a promise to a Jew ?
Dispatches printed in *The Times*

The Star Gazette and *Daily News*

MARCHANT
The Chronicle IS MINE !

PENNELL
The Post and *New Age* fall !

MARCHANT
The Post is a load of balls !

MARCHANT / PENNELL [together]
The slag has stabbed me in the back !/ Why keep a promise to a Jew ?

PENNELL
The tramp has got a poisoned pen !
Pah!
New York will publish any shit
I'd better use a *nom de plume !*

MARCHANT
A cowardly pseudonym !

PENNELL
I got him on the floor
Now kick him when he's down !

MARCHANT / PENNELL [together]
The slag has stabbed me in the back ! /Why keep a promise to a Jew ?

MARCHANT
Hypocrite !
Anyway my money's made ! Hah !

PENNELL
At last my labours are bearing fruit
Sales of Greaves's paintings have stopped dead... floundering in a sea of uncertainty

MARCHANT
[Hums a tune]
Not a bad little show by any standard !

PENNELL
Hasn't had a sale in days...The bubble's burst !

MARCHANT
Hmmm Twelve thousand eight hundred...thirteen thousand... three hundred and fifty..

PENNELL
We gotta bury him !
That's the way Whistler would go at it !

MARCHANT
Fourteen thousand one hundred...and fifty...this is very nice...two hundred and forty...

PENNELL
I'll follow to the kill...even if I go down with them
Greaves goes back in the gutter or I...

MARCHANT
Of course Pennell is a guttersnipe !

PENNELL
Every reference to Greaves must be re-written for the Fifth Edition !

MARCHANT/ PENNELL [together]
Now I'll just pop out and throw this lot in the post at Piccadilly !
[THEY collide at the post-box]

MARCHANT
So sorry !

BOTH
AAAAAGH !

[BLACKOUT.
GREAVES knocks timidly at MARCHANT 's door.]

MARCHANT
Come !

GREAVES
'Morning

MARCHANT
Ah Walter ! How are you ?

GREAVES
Not bad... not bad

MARCHANT
I have to apologise for getting angry with you last time we....

GREAVES
Eh ? Oh that !
I like to see a man letting off a head of steam now and then... does him good
Can't do it myself of course
....
Mr Marchant... see this letter I gets from the Midland Bank this morning ?
They'll be paying me thirty shillings a week
I don't understand

MARCHANT
I know it's very little but....

GREAVES
Tinnie and me's not your responsibility...we never wanted you to think we was

MARCHANT
At the outset I told you there's be something in it for you

GREAVES
No no no...
Ay... they bought several bits and pieces down in Chelsea last week... even one of the oils
They never bought the oils down there in the old days

MARCHANT
That's wonderful !

GREAVES
This business with Mrs Pennell in the papers 'as put a damper on it mind
Expect it'll pick up later eh ?

MARCHANT
I hope you're asking a proper price

GREAVES
Oh yes... two pounds for the big oils thirty shillin's for....

MARCHANT
You're mad !!!

GREAVES
That's my real life down there
The pub... the river... old neighbours
Them people kept me alive this past thirty years

MARCHANT
Kept you alive !

GREAVES
Kept alive is quite important when you're not sure of it Mr Marchant

MARCHANT
Oh well...
How is Tinnie ?

GREAVES

Poorly enough... The chest was always the weakness...couldn't take the cold nohow...

She'd love to see you

Do her good to see a young face now and then

MARCHANT

Flatterer !

..I'll try to run out and see her very soon !

.....

Well Walter... I'm about to close the exhibition

We certainly whipped up a bit of a stir on the London Art scene eh ?

GREAVES

Didn't we half !

Surprised a few people an' all...

GREAVES

There's a wonderful tribute to you here in the *New Age* from Walter Sickert...keep that copy

He says your *Race Day On Battersea Bridge* is a masterpiece... compares it with Carpaccio !

Sickert says so many beautiful things about you

GREAVES

Oh my !

MARCHANT

Makes the whole wrangle with Mrs Pennell worth while. Even th... You have brought out the best and the worst thing in this city Greaves...

GREAVES

I never wished to hurt no one

MARCHANT

It'll be some time before I can sell any more Greaveses

But y'know...Mrs Pennell has damaged Whistler's reputation more than yours
She's gone against her own book...
Said you've painted several "Whistlers" in public collections

GREAVES
Don't let's talk about Mrs Pennell

MARCHANT
I like to understand what makes people tick

GREAVES
I'm some kind of coward... always avoid anger... run away from it
....
This exhibition you done....it's given something...a what would you say ?
...an explanation...to me... why I lived... Aw I'm not saying this right...
I hope financially it ain't hurt you too bad... all them letters to the papers and all...

MARCHANT
I made quite a lot of money from this exhibition
It's stopped now.... but the whole venture has been an extraordinary success
Your name is intact... it'll grow when this settles down... you've gone into public collections

GREAVES
Bit frightening that

MARCHANT
I mean... the fashionable set may turn to something else... they do anyway
The great thing is the impression you have made on the young painters
Augustus John... Bill Nicholson.... they'll carry your influence into another era...

GREAVES
Oh dear.... you think so ? My influence

MARCHANT
Yes

GREAVES
Something to think about eh ?
.....
Now I'll toddle along Mr Marchant

MARCHANT
My studio is here for you to work in... you know that

GREAVES
Ah no... I prefer to work down the Thames
Though I got every ripple every house every boat and change of light here in me old head !
But I do like to make sure no one's run off with me pub ! Heh heh heh !
Get in to see Tinnie if you can !

MARCHANT
I'll try

[Exit GREAVES .
Agitated entrance of JOHN.]

JOHN
MARCHANT !

MARCHANT
Augustus ! How are you ?

JOHN
Angry !

MARCHANT
Angry ? Who is the unfortunate ...?

JOHN
You ! I'm angry with you !...You've treated Greaves shamefully !

MARCHANT
Whatever are you talking about ?

JOHN
Thirty shillings ! I know what I'd tell you to do with your thirty shillings !

MARCHANT
He wanted nothing ! I insisted !
Now you listen... thirty shillings is a lot of money to one of Greaves's class
He's well able to work and I...

JOHN
He is a great artist and a beautiful human being
Greaves need to be protected see and you pick his carcase like a bloody vulture
I'm just physically sick of the whole affair
You've raked in about twenty thousand in a couple of weeks on that man's life 's work
Thirty shillings !

MARCHANT
The overheads here... you'd be surprised how...

JOHN
Lined your damned pockets and flung him back in the gutter !

MARCHANT
You want him and that crazy sister of his to drink themselves to death on my money ?
That's all they'd do with it !

JOHN
And if they did itself what business of yours is it ?

MARCHANT
It was my business head that dragged him from the gutter
Gave meaning to his empty squandered life !

JOHN
The only thing you understand is money
In money terms you treated him like shite !
That's the measure of you man !
And if it's all done in the name of "Art"
You drop the odd crumb to the poor artist and grow fat on his sweating !

MARCHANT
Really ?
Money is the grist that life is made of
I have to live... I have to pay my way !
You're doing well yourself... that makes you guilty doesn't it ?
Well go and settle some of on him !

JOHN
BOLLOCKS !!

MARCHANT
No ? Too close to the bone isn't it ?
Easier to grow fat and preach altruism to me !
That's the measure of you John ! And if it's all done for the "poor artist"
And against the "wicked art dealer"... so much the better !

JOHN
DESPICABLE !

MARCHANT
Those pictures were all mine... I paid what I was asked for them !

JOHN
HAH !

MARCHANT
He's grateful to me...grateful and proud !
Anyway if he can get back to his good work
I'll give him another exhibition in three or four years time..

JOHN
You want to suck his blood till he's in the grave !

MARCHANT
He doesn't value his own work... why only......

JOHN
Right ! And you value it solely for your own profit !

MARCHANT
If I didn't make a profit artists would starve

JOHN
You do and they still starve !

MARCHANT
Go out and start a fund for indigent artists if you wish Augustus
I'm just an ordinary businessman... I'm not trying to change the world !
I give to charity...

JOHN
The devil take you and charity !
You are inhuman and unnatural !

MARCHANT
If you believe that you simply do not understand human nature !

JOHN
This I do understand... Greaves deserves love and shelter from the cold winds
That howl through this money-grubbing city !

MARCHANT
Too much shelter weakens the Greaveses of this world !
The wind isn't always howling
And they come up straight and strong when it falls !
Leave them to their struggle Augustus...
Unless you are prepared to look after them for good !

I know you...This week it's the Greaveses... next week it'll be stray dogs
Now I must get this exhibition organised if you'll....

JOHN
You frighten me Marchant... full of wisdom aren't you ?

MARCHANT
We live in a competitive world John... winners and losers
I work hard balance my books... I save a little
It's very simple...good housekeeping hard work and a logical approach
Greaves is free as I am to do the same...

JOHN
Full of the wisdom of Hell !

[Storms out.
BLACKOUT on MARCHANT .
The Embankment....Winter.
GREAVES, cold, hopelessly
trying to interest passers-by in his work.
Unrecognised and unrecognising
PENNELL as she waits for JOHN.]

GREAVES
Fancy one of these lady ?... All good work !
A pupil of Whistler's I was...
[Exit GREAVES . Enter JOHN]

JOHN
That black wind howls up the Embankment from the frozen steppes of Russia !
Come to the studio for God's sake !

PENNELL
I want to talk

JOHN
There's a decent fire in The Kings Head

PENNELL
I will not be seen in a public house !

JOHN
I must get off the streets...there's an assassin out to do for me !

PENNELL
You have no respect for me !

JOHN
I love you Lizzy !

PENNELL
Ahhh maybe you do... maybe you do in your fashion
Where have you been ?

JOHN
Dorset

PENNELL
Liar
Who is the lucky woman this time ?

JOHN
I've been on a binge... I don't know where I've been

PENNELL
Everyone else does
There was a sixteen-year-old tart in The Café Royal yesterday
Reading a nine-page love letter from you
Her audience was half of London society !
If she only knew how you'll use her as you use every woman you get into your clutches !

JOHN
Women use me

PENNELL
I need stability

JOHN

Dear God ! I lay the world at her feet and she asks for the moon !
Stability !
Who is that man by Carlyle's statue ?

PENNELL

I am no longer amused or alarmed by you phantasy about an assassin !

JOHN

She... The Walking Hell-Bitch of The Western World
Has hired some desperado to... To cut my throat actually...

PENNELL

Rubbish ! Madame Strindberg is a sophisticated and cultured woman

JOHN

He left a man for dead down by Sloan Square on Saturday night...
mistook him for me
She told me so herself.... That woman is my Nemesis !

PENNELL

Go to the police

JOHN

An artist has no business getting mixed up with the Law
Come to my warm studio and make love with me Lizzy !
It's the only thing we're any good at

PENNELL

We are good at a great many things...especially you
Even good at parting...

JOHN

Don't !

PENNELL

...So we are going to part in the most civilised way imaginable...

JOHN
I AM NOT CIVILISED !

PENNELL
You have wooed me with all the subtlety of a prize bull !

JOHN
I am nothing I don't admit to

PENNELL
Here on Chelsea Embankment
Standing among the ghosts of a hundred artists I make this vow
I shall never meet you alone again
Goodbye Mr John

[SHE offers her hand which
He brushes aside.]

That was the Quaker-girl
....
Goodbye my beauty ! Oh GOD !

[SHE throws herself briefly into JOHN's arms
breaks violently away and exits running.
BLACKOUT
Greaves's home. TINNIE ill and lying down.
WALTER nearby.]

TINNIE
Things is near as bad as before
I'll never be well again

GREAVES
Sssh

TINNIE
Brought you down again I 'ave

GREAVES
I ain't brought down
We can't never starve now

TINNIE [Coughs}
Dear god... it's difficult... trying to die and not be a burden to no one

GREAVES
Don't say that
I'll get you well...See if I don't eh ?

TINNIE
What day is it ?

GREAVES
Tuesday

TINNIE
Aw... three days till your money comes
Thirty shillings don't go far these days does it love ?
Is there anything left for your supper ?

GREAVES
I kept some of that beef tea for you

TINNIE
You have it... I'm too tired

GREAVES
I'll make it do the both of us... all right ?

TINNIE
Good
Well at least I'm dying in a decent bed...
Jesus the shame of dying on the floor in a heap of rags...like a dog...used to haunt me

GREAVES
It can't happen now

TINNIE
You so sure ?

'''

Walter...

GREAVES

Eh ?

TINNIE

I been thinking

GREAVES

I'll get some bread on the slate maybe

TINNIE

Thinking of the lonely years...

GREAVES

I saw a big potato on the street yesterday... when the vegetable barrow moved off...

TINNIE

How could he know... the power and all-consuming fire he lit in me...

GREAVES

I'll stroll around that way this evening

<u>TINNIE</u>

<u>You're to sell the rest of Jimmy's letters !</u>

GREAVES

Aw don't upset yourself with that again... we been over it a thousand times !

TINNIE

I want them out of the house

Take them to Miss Spencer and get her to sell them for you

GREAVES

Not at this stage

I'll not open our private things to the world... not just for money
I want to keep some... something

TINNIE
Foolish vanity and pride always !
I've no time for that now ! [Fit of coughing]
God I'm done for !

GREAVES
Stop !

TINNIE
Who's to pay the doctor ?

GREAVES
We'll manage

TINNIE
And them tonics ?

GREAVES
We'll manage

TINNIE
Do what I ask now in the name of God
And don't go against me on my dying bed !

GREAVES
Tinnie... you don't want them intimate things passed round as public property

TINNIE
What is it to me and they're public property ?
Just let me die in peace that's all I ask !
Anyways why shouldn't the world know what I was to Whistler... and you too for that matter
Let the world know should he have made me his wife !

GREAVES
These are all I have from the old times...

TINNIE
Every word a dagger in my heart

GREAVES
I wouldn't want to lose the memories

TINNIE
Would to Christ I could then !
Day and night I hear them cursed letters... silver tongue...
whisperin'...whisperin'..
"my dearest Tinnie...my life my dream my jewel my love...
Touch...let me touch you again my sweet my naughty Tinnie...."

GREAVES
STOP IT !! I WON!T LISTEN TO IT !
I should have burned them ! BURNED THEM

TINNIE [Fit of coughing]
GET THE MONEY FOR THEM WALTER ! We don't need them no more
My head is full of the sound of them ! Please do it !

GREAVES
Eh ?
You say something ?

TINNIE
For me...at least go and ask Spencer what the letters is worth...in case of emergency
Then we'd know wouldn't we ?... If only to bury me...

GREAVES
Tinnie !

TINNIE
We got to think on these things... I don't want to lie in no paupers' field..

Now go... see what she says

GREAVES
Well...........just ask ?

TINNIE
You're a good brother to me
....
Walter

GREAVES
Hmm ?

TINNIE
Lie beside me !

GREAVES
Aw Tinnie !

TINNIE
I'm cold as the grave....Come

GREAVES
......
Just for a minute then

TINNIE
Hold me... just for the last little minute...

[LIGHTS down.
Cuckoo clock strikes.
GREAVES with SPENCER.]

GREAVES
Maybe I've come at a bad time Miss Spencer

SPENCER
No no ...hmmm really interesting... beautiful...beautiful

There's nothing like this ever come on the market as you probably realise
Does Mrs Pennell know ?

GREAVES
Nobody only Tinnie and me... they're very private

SPENCER
Of course...
This eh ...Tinnie ?

GREAVES
Yes

SPENCER
Whistler was...

GREAVES
Well you can see can't you ?

SPENCER
I'm just wondering whom to offer them to...
We'll get a lot of money for these

GREAVES
Yes ?

SPENCER
I would take five shillings in the pound commission
But you'd still be getting many hundreds... don't hold me to a figure now...

GREAVES
Oh my goodness..we never dreamed...

SPENCER
They are quite eh explicit... they will attract a great deal of attention
That whole area of Whistler's life is..or was... clouded in mystery
A lot of talk but no clear evidence
Here we would have...Are you all right Mr Greaves ?

GREAVES
Dear me... this is a puzzlement

SPENCER
You should consult your sister about it

GREAVES
NO... she's been pressing me to come to you

SPENCER
Then there's no problem !
Mr Greaves you may prepare yourself for the limelight again !
Let me give you a hundred pounds right away...

GREAVES
Heavens ! You business people talk in such....
I don't know what to say... these letters is very private...personal

SPENCER
That's why they are so important... so valuable

GREAVES
Yes ?

SPENCER
They could be published almost as they stand...

GREAVES
Well... oh dear... I must think about this.... so private

SPENCER
Think about it for a few days... consult someone
Marchant would advice you sensibly...he's been a good friend to you

GREAVES
No. I'll... now...I'll decide now
Let me see them again please
....

Oh my we loved each other so much in them days..... Jimmy Tinnie...me ......
Magic
They're really so private.....but Tinnie needs things see...

SPENCER
Of course
But you know the money's here if you...

GREAVES
We ain't starving...not like before

SPENCER
I can see you have the greatest difficulty selling such treasures...for money
A great temptation isn't it ?

GREAVES
Such a temptation....

[GREAVES is leaving]

When you're poor...

[GREAVES is heading towards his beloved river as SPENCER follows a little way.]

SPENCER
Mr Greaves ! Mr Greaves !

[GREAVES nearing the river
Cries of seabirds.
JENNY as CHESTNUT SELLER approaching.]

JENNY
Chestnuts ! 'Ot Chestnuts !

GREAVES
When you're poor...such a temptation..
All the lonely years
How could he know the power and all-consuming fire he lit in me...

JENNY
Chestnuts ! Hot chestnuts mate ?
....
Cat got your tongue then ?

[No reply from GREAVES who is setting fire
to his precious letters at the chestnut brazier-barrow.]

Ay there old mate... not burnin' yer old love-letters are yah ?

GREAVES
Yes... I'm burning them
....
Such temptation

[JENNY laughs silently as
GREAVES goes down to the river.
Seabirds' cries and sounds of water lapping
as the ashes blow from his trembling fingers
and settle on the silent drifts of the Thames.]

GREAVES
[Agony] JIMMY !

[FINAL SLOW BLACKOUT.]

www.ingramcontent.com/pod-product-compliance
Ingram Content Group UK Ltd.
Pitfield, Milton Keynes, MK11 3LW, UK
UKHW020158200726
13856UKWH00003B/1065

9 781847 536990